C000296830

SAKI'S CATS

TOBERMORY

IT WAS A CHILL, RAIN-WASHED afternoon of a late August day, that indefinite season when partridges are still in security or cold storage, and there is nothing to hunt – unless one is bounded on the north by the Bristol Channel, in which case one may lawfully gallop after fat red stags. Lady Blemley's house party was not bounded on the north by the Bristol Channel, hence there was a full gathering of her guests round the tea table on this particular afternoon. And, in spite of the blankness of the season and the triteness of the occasion,

there was no trace in the company of that
fatigued restlessness which means a dread
of the pianola and a subdued hankering
for auction bridge. The undisguised open-
mouthed attention of the entire party was
fixed on the homely negative personality of
Mr Cornelius Appin. Of all her guests, he
was the one who had come to Lady Blemley
with the vaguest reputation. Someone had
said he was 'clever', and he had got his invitation in the moderate expectation, on
the part of his hostess, that some portion, at
least, of his cleverness would be contributed
to the general entertainment. Until teatime
that day she had been unable to discover in
what direction, if any, his cleverness lay. He
was neither a wit nor a croquet champion,
a hypnotic force nor a begetter of amateur
theatricals. Neither did his exterior suggest
the sort of man in whom women are will-
ing to pardon a generous measure of mental deficiency. He had subsided into mere

Mr Appin, and the Cornelius seemed a piece of transparent baptismal bluff. And now he was claiming to have launched on the world a discovery beside which the invention of gunpowder, of the printing press and of steam locomotion were inconsiderable trifles. Science had made bewildering strides in many directions during recent decades, but this thing seemed to belong to the domain of miracle rather than to scientific achievement.

'And do you really ask us to believe,' Sir Wilfrid was saying, 'that you have discovered a means for instructing animals in the art of human speech, and that dear old Tobermory has proved your first successful pupil?'

'It is a problem at which I have worked for the last seventeen years,' said Mr Appin, 'but only during the last eight or nine months have I been rewarded with glimmerings of success. Of course, I have experimented

11

with thousands of animals, but latterly only with cats – those wonderful creatures which have assimilated themselves so marvellously with our civilisation, while retaining all their highly developed feral instincts. Here and there among cats one comes across an outstanding superior intellect, just as one does among the ruck of human beings, and when I made the acquaintance of Tobermory a week ago I saw at once that I was in contact with a "Beyond-cat" of extraordinary intelligence. I had gone far along the road to success in recent experiments; with Tobermory, as you call him, I have reached the goal.'

Mr Appin concluded his remarkable statement in a voice which he strove to divest of a triumphant inflection. No one said 'rats', though Clovis' lips moved in a monosyllabic contortion which probably invoked those rodents of disbelief.

'And do you mean to say,' asked Miss Resker, after a slight pause, 'that you have taught Tobermory to say and understand easy sentences of one syllable?'

'My dear Miss Resker,' said the wonder-worker patiently, 'one teaches little children and savages and backward adults in that piecemeal fashion; when one has once solved the problem of making a beginning with an animal of highly developed intelligence, one has no need for those halting methods. Tobermory can speak our language with perfect correctness.'

This time Clovis very distinctly said, 'Beyond-rats!' Sir Wilfrid was more polite, but equally sceptical.

'Hadn't we better have the cat in and judge for ourselves?' suggested Lady Blemley.

Sir Wilfrid went in search of the animal, and the company settled themselves down to the languid expectation of witnessing some more or less adroit drawing-room ventriloquism.

In a minute Sir Wilfrid was back in the room, his face white beneath its tan and his eyes dilated with excitement.

'By Gad, it's true!'

His agitation was unmistakably genuine, and his hearers started forward in a thrill of awakened interest.

Collapsing into an armchair, he continued breathlessly: 'I found him dozing in the smoking room, and called out to him to come for his tea. He blinked at me in his usual way, and I said, "Come on, Toby; don't keep us waiting" – and, by Gad! He drawled out in a most horribly natural voice that he'd come when he dashed well pleased! I nearly jumped out of my skin!'

Appin had preached to absolutely incredulous hearers; Sir Wilfrid's statement carried instant conviction. A Babel-like chorus of startled exclamation arose, amid which the scientist sat mutely enjoying the first fruit of his stupendous discovery.

In the midst of the clamour, Tobermory entered the room and made his way with velvet tread and studied unconcern across to the group seated round the tea table.

A sudden hush of awkwardness and constraint fell on the company. Somehow there seemed an element of embarrassment in addressing on equal terms a domestic cat of acknowledged mental ability.

'Will you have some milk, Tobermory?' asked Lady Blemley in a rather strained voice.

'I don't mind if I do,' was the response, couched in a tone of even indifference. A shiver of suppressed excitement went through the listeners, and Lady Blemley might be excused for pouring out the saucerful of milk rather unsteadily.

'I'm afraid I've spilled a good deal of it,' she said apologetically.

'After all, it's not my Axminster,' was Tobermory's rejoinder.

Another silence fell on the group, and then Miss Resker, in her best district-visitor manner, asked if the human language had been difficult to learn. Tobermory looked squarely at her for a moment and then fixed his gaze serenely on the middle distance. It was obvious that boring questions lay outside his scheme of life.

'What do you think of human intelligence?' asked Mavis Pellington lamely.

'Of whose intelligence in particular?' asked Tobermory coldly.

'Oh, well, mine, for instance,' said Mavis, with a feeble laugh.

'You put me in an embarrassing position,' said Tobermory, whose tone and attitude certainly did not suggest a shred of embarrassment. 'When your inclusion in this house party was suggested, Sir Wilfrid protested that you were the most brainless woman of his acquaintance, and that there was a wide distinction between hospitality and the care of the feeble-minded. Lady Blemley replied that your lack of brain-power was the precise quality which had earned you your invitation, as you were the only person she could think of who might be idiotic enough to buy their old car. You know, the one they call "The Envy of Sisyphus"* because it goes quite nicely uphill if you push it.'

Lady Blemley's protestations would have had greater effect if she had not casually suggested to Mavis only that morning that the car in question would be just the thing for her down at her Devonshire home.

Major Barfield plunged in heavily to effect a diversion.

'How about your carryings-on with the tortoiseshell puss up at the stables, eh?'

The moment he had said it everyone realised the blunder.

'One does not usually discuss these matters in public,' said Tobermory, frigidly.

'From a slight observation of your ways since you've been in this house, I should imagine you'd find it inconvenient if I were to shift the conversation on to your own little affairs.'

The panic which ensued was not confined to the Major.

'Would you like to go and see if cook has got your dinner ready?' suggested Lady Blemley hurriedly, affecting to ignore the fact that it wanted at least two hours to Tobermory's dinnertime.

'Thanks,' said Tobermory, 'not quite so soon after my tea. I don't want to die of indigestion.'

'Cats have nine lives, you know,' said Sir Wilfrid heartily.

'Possibly,' answered Tobermory, 'but only one liver.'

'Adelaide!' said Mrs Cornett, 'Do you mean to encourage that cat to go out and gossip about us in the servants' hall?'

The panic had indeed become general. A narrow ornamental balustrade ran in front of most of the bedroom windows at the Towers, and it was recalled with dismay that this had formed a favourite promenade for Tobermory at all hours, whence he could watch the pigeons – and Heaven knew what else besides. If he intended to become reminiscent in his present outspoken strain, the effect would be something more than disconcerting. Mrs Cornett, who spent much time at her toilet table, and whose complexion was reputed to be of a nomadic though punctual disposition, looked as ill at ease as the Major. Miss Scrawen, who wrote fiercely sensuous poetry and led a blameless life, merely displayed irritation – if you are methodical and virtuous in private you don't necessarily want everyone to know it. Bertie van Tahn, who was so depraved at seventeen that he had long ago given up trying to be any worse, turned a dull shade of gardenia white, but he did not commit the error of dashing out of the room like Odo Finsberry, a young gentleman who was understood to be reading for the Church and who was possibly disturbed at the thought of scandals he might hear concerning other people. Clovis had the presence of mind to maintain a composed exterior; privately he was calculating how long it would take to procure a box of fancy mice through the agency of the *Exchange and Mart** as a species of hush money.

Even in a delicate situation like the present, Agnes Resker could not endure to remain too long in the background.

'Why did I ever come down here?' she asked dramatically.

Tobermory immediately accepted the opening.

'Judging by what you said to Mrs Cornett on the croquet lawn yesterday, you were

out for food. You described the Blemleys
as the dullest people to stay with that you
knew, but said they were clever enough to
employ a first-rate cook – otherwise they'd
find it difficult to get anyone to come down
a second time.'

'There's not a word of truth in it! I ap-
peal to Mrs Cornett...' exclaimed the dis-
comfited Agnes.

'Mrs Cornett repeated your remark afterwards to Bertie van Tahn,' continued
Tobermory, 'and said, "That woman is a
regular Hunger Marcher; she'd go any-
where for four square meals a day," and
Bertie van Tahn said...'

At this point the chronicle mercifully
ceased. Tobermory had caught a glimpse
of the big yellow tom from the rectory
working his way through the shrubbery
towards the stable wing. In a flash he had
vanished through the open French windows.

With the disappearance of his too-brilliant pupil, Cornelius Appin found himself beset by a hurricane of bitter upbraiding, anxious inquiry and frightened entreaty. The responsibility for the situation lay with him, and he must prevent matters from becoming worse. 'Could Tobermory impart his dangerous gift to other cats?' was the first question he had to answer. It was possible, he replied, that he might have initiated his intimate friend the stable puss into his new accomplishment, but it was unlikely that his teaching could have taken a wider range as yet.

'Then,' said Mrs Cornett, 'Tobermory may be a valuable cat and a great pet, but I'm sure you'll agree, Adelaide, that both he and the stable cat must be done away with without delay.'

'You don't suppose I've enjoyed the last quarter of an hour, do you?' said Lady Blemley bitterly. 'My husband and I are very fond of Tobermory – at least, we were, before this horrible accomplishment was infused into him – but now, of course, the only thing is to have him destroyed as soon as possible.'

'We can put some strychnine in the scraps he always gets at dinnertime,' said Sir Wilfrid, 'and I will go and drown the stable cat myself. The coachman will be very sore at losing his pet, but I'll say a very catching form of mange has broken out in both cats and we're afraid of its spreading to the kennels.'

'But my great discovery!' expostulated Mr Appin. 'After all my years of research and experiment—'

'You can go and experiment on the short-horns at the farm, who are under proper control,' said Mrs Cornett, 'or the elephants at the Zoological Gardens. They're said to be highly intelligent, and they have this recommendation: that they don't come creeping about our bedrooms and under chairs, and so forth.'

An archangel ecstatically proclaiming the millennium, and then finding that it clashed unpardonably with Henley* and would have to be indefinitely postponed, could hardly have felt more crestfallen than Cornelius Appin at the reception of his wonderful achievement. Public opinion, however, was against him – in fact, had the general voice been consulted on the subject, it is probable that a strong minority vote would have been in favour of including him in the strychnine diet.

Defective train arrangements and a nervous desire to see matters brought to a finish prevented an immediate dispersal of the party, but dinner that evening was not a social success. Sir Wilfrid had had rather a trying time with the stable cat, and subsequently with the coachman. Agnes Resker ostentatiously limited her repast to a morsel of dry toast, which she bit as though it were a personal enemy, while Mavis Pellington maintained a vindictive silence throughout the meal. Lady Blemley kept up a flow of what she hoped was conversation, but her attention was fixed on the doorway. A plateful of carefully dosed fish scraps was in readiness on the sideboard, but sweets and savoury and dessert went their way, and no Tobermory appeared either in the dining room or kitchen.

The sepulchral dinner was cheerful compared with the subsequent vigil in the smoking room. Eating and drinking had at least supplied a distraction and cloak to the prevailing embarrassment. Bridge was out of the question in the general tension of nerves and tempers, and after Odo Finsberry had given a lugubrious rendering of *Mélisande in the Wood** to a frigid audience, music was tacitly avoided. At eleven the servants went to bed, announcing that the small window in the pantry had been left open as usual for Tobermory's private use. The guests read steadily through the current batch of magazines, and fell back gradually on the *Badminton Library* and bound volumes of *Punch*.* Lady Blemley made periodic visits to the pantry, returning each time with an expression of listless depression which forestalled questioning.

At two o'clock Clovis broke the dominating silence.

'He won't turn up tonight. He's probably in the local newspaper office at the present moment, dictating the first instalment of his reminiscences. Lady What's-her-name's book won't be in it. It will be the event of the day.'

Having made this contribution to the general cheerfulness, Clovis went to bed. At long intervals the various members of the house party followed his example.

The servants taking round the early tea made a uniform announcement in reply to a uniform question. Tobermory had not returned.

Breakfast was, if anything, a more unpleasant function than dinner had been, but before its conclusion the situation was relieved. Tobermory's corpse was brought in from the shrubbery, where a gardener had just discovered it. From the bites on his throat and the yellow fur which coated his claws it was evident that he had fallen in unequal combat with the big tom from the rectory.

By midday most of the guests had quitted the Towers, and after lunch Lady Blemley had sufficiently recovered her spirits to write an extremely nasty letter to the rectory about the loss of her valuable pet.

Tobermory had been Appin's one successful pupil, and he was destined to have no successor. A few weeks later an elephant in the Dresden Zoological Garden, which had shown no previous signs of irritability, broke loose and killed an Englishman who had apparently been teasing it. The victim's name was variously reported in the papers as Oppin and Eppelin, but his front name was faithfully rendered Cornelius.

'If he was trying German irregular verbs on the poor beast,' said Clovis, 'he deserved all he got.'

THE PHILANTHROPIST AND

THE HAPPY CAT

JOCANTHA BESSBURY was in the mood to be serenely and graciously happy. Her world was a pleasant place, and it was wearing one of its pleasantest aspects. Gregory had managed to get home for a hurried lunch and a smoke afterwards in the little snuggery; the lunch had been a good one, and there was just time to do justice to the coffee and cigarettes. Both were excellent in their way, and Gregory was, in his way, an excellent husband. Jocantha rather suspected herself of making him a very charming wife, and more than suspected herself of having a first-rate dressmaker.

'I don't suppose a more thoroughly contented personality is to be found in all Chelsea,' observed Jocantha in allusion to herself; 'except perhaps Attab,' she continued, glancing towards the large tabby-marked cat that lay in considerable ease in a corner of the divan. 'He lies there, purring and dreaming, shifting his limbs now and then in an ecstasy of cushioned comfort. He seems the incarnation of everything soft and silky and velvety, without a sharp edge in his composition, a dreamer whose philosophy is sleep and let sleep; and then, as evening draws on, he goes out into the garden with a red glint in his eyes and slays a drowsy sparrow.'

'As every pair of sparrows hatches out ten or more young ones in the year, while their food supply remains stationary, it is just as well that the Attabs of the community should have that idea of how to pass an amusing afternoon,' said Gregory. Having delivered himself of this sage comment, he lit another cigarette, bade Jocantha a playfully affectionate goodbye and departed into the outer world.

'Remember, dinner's a wee bit earlier tonight, as we're going to the Haymarket,' she called after him.

Left to herself, Jocantha continued the process of looking at her life with placid, introspective eyes. If she had not everything she wanted in this world, at least she was very well pleased with what she had got. She was very well pleased, for instance, with the snuggery, which contrived somehow to be cosy and dainty and expensive all at once. The porcelain was rare and beautiful, the Chinese enamels took on wonderful tints in the firelight, the rugs and hangings led the eye through sumptuous harmonies of colouring. It was a room in which one might have

31

suitably entertained an ambassador or an archbishop, but it was also a room in which one could cut out pictures for a scrapbook without feeling that one was scandalising the deities of the place with one's litter. And as with the snuggery, so with the rest of the house; and as with the house, so with the other departments of Jocantha's life; she really had good reason for being one of the most contented women in Chelsea.

From being in a mood of simmering satisfaction with her lot, she passed to the phase of being generously commiserating for those thousands around her whose lives and circumstances were dull, cheap, pleasureless and empty. Work girls, shop assistants and so forth – the class that have neither the happy-go-lucky freedom of the poor nor the leisured freedom of the rich – came specially within the range of her sympathy. It was sad to think that there were young people who, after a long day's work, had to sit alone in chill, dreary bedrooms because they could not afford the price of a cup of coffee and a sandwich in a restaurant – still less a shilling for a theatre gallery.

Jocantha's mind was still dwelling on this theme when she started forth on an afternoon campaign of desultory shopping; it would be rather a comforting thing, she told herself, if she could do something, on the spur of the moment, to bring a gleam of pleasure and interest into the life of even one or two wistful-hearted, empty-pocketed workers; it would add a good deal to her sense of enjoyment at the theatre that night. She would get two upper circle tickets for a popular play, make her way into some cheap tea shop and present the tickets to the first couple of interesting work girls with whom she could casually drop into conversation. She could explain matters by saying that she was unable to use the tickets herself and did not want them to be wasted, and, on the other hand, did not want the trouble of sending them back. On further reflection, she decided that it might be better to get only one ticket and give it to some lonely-looking girl sitting eating her frugal meal by herself; the girl might scrape acquaintance with her next-seat neighbour at the theatre and lay the foundations of a lasting friendship.

With the fairy-godmother impulse strong upon her, Jocantha marched into a ticket agency and selected with immense care an upper circle seat for the *Yellow Peacock* – a play that was attracting a considerable amount of discussion and criticism. Then she went forth in search of a tea shop and philanthropic adventure, at about the same time that Attab sauntered into the garden with a mind attuned to sparrow stalking. In a corner of an ABC shop* she found an unoccupied table, whereat she promptly installed herself, impelled by the fact that at the next table was sitting a young girl, rather plain of feature,

34

with tired, listless eyes and a general air of uncomplaining forlornness. Her dress was of poor material, but aimed at being in the fashion; her hair was pretty, and her complexion bad; she was finishing a modest meal of tea and scone, and she was not very different in her way from thousands of other girls who were finishing, or beginning, or continuing their teas in London tea shops at that exact moment. The odds were enormously in favour of the supposition that she had never seen the *Yellow Peacock*; obviously she supplied excellent material for Jocantha's first experiment in haphazard benefaction.

Jocantha ordered some tea and a muffin, and then turned a friendly scrutiny on her neighbour with a view to catching her eye. At that precise moment the girl's face lit up with sudden pleasure, her eyes sparkled, a flush came into her cheeks and she looked almost pretty. A young man, whom she greeted with an affectionate 'Hullo, Bertie', came up to her table and took his seat in a chair facing her. Jocantha looked hard at the newcomer; he was in appearance a few years younger than herself, very much better looking than Gregory – rather better looking, in fact, than any of the young men of her set. She guessed him to be a well-mannered young clerk in some wholesale warehouse, existing and amusing himself as best he might on a tiny salary, and commanding a holiday of about two weeks in the year. He was aware, of course, of his good looks, but with the shy self-consciousness of the Anglo-Saxon, not the blatant complacency of the Latin or Semite. He was obviously on terms of friendly intimacy with the girl he was talking to – probably they were drifting towards a formal engagement. Jocantha pictured the boy's home, in a rather narrow circle, with a tiresome mother who always wanted to know how and where he spent his evenings. He would exchange that humdrum thraldom in due course for a home of his own, dominated by a chronic scarcity of pounds, shillings and pence, and a dearth of most of the things that made life attractive or comfortable. Jocantha felt extremely sorry for him. She wondered if he had seen the *Yellow Peacock*; the odds were enormously in favour of the supposition that he had not. The girl had finished her tea, and would shortly be going back to her work; when the boy was alone it would be quite easy for Jocantha to say: 'My husband has made other arrangements for me this evening; would you care to make use of this ticket, which would otherwise be wasted?' Then she could come there again one afternoon for tea, and, if she saw him, ask him how he liked the play. If he was a nice boy and improved on acquaintance, he could be given more theatre tickets and perhaps asked to come one Sunday to tea at Chelsea. Jocantha made up her mind that he would improve on acquaintance, and that Gregory would like him, and that the fairy-godmother business would prove far more entertaining than she had originally anticipated. The boy was distinctly presentable; he knew how to brush his hair, which was possibly an imitative faculty; he knew what colour of tie suited him, which might be intuition; he was exactly the type that Jocantha admired, which, of course, was accident. Altogether she was rather pleased when the girl looked at the clock and bade a friendly but hurried farewell to her companion. Bertie nodded 'goodbye', gulped down a mouthful of tea and then produced from his overcoat pocket a paper-covered book bearing the title *Sepoy and Sahib, a Tale of the Great Mutiny*.

The laws of tea-shop etiquette forbid that you should offer theatre tickets to a stranger without having first caught the stranger's eye. It is even better if you can ask to have a sugar basin passed to you, having previously concealed the fact that you have a large and well-filled sugar basin on your own table; this is not difficult to manage, as the printed menu is generally nearly as large as the table, and can be made to stand on end. Jocantha set to work hopefully: she had a long and rather high-pitched discussion with the waitress concerning alleged defects in an altogether blameless muffin; she made loud and plaint-ive enquiries about the tube service to some impossibly remote suburb; she talked with brilliant insincerity to the tea-shop kitten; and as a last resort she upset a milk jug and swore at it daintily. Altogether she attracted a good deal of attention, but never for a moment did she attract the attention of the boy with the beautifully brushed hair, who was some thousands of miles away in the baking plains of Hindustan, amid deserted bungalows, seething bazaars and riotous barrack squares, listening to the throbbing of tom-toms and the distant rattle of musketry.

Jocantha went back to her house in Chelsea, which struck her for the first time as looking dull and over-furnished. She had a resentful conviction that Gregory would be uninteresting at dinner, and that the play would be stupid after dinner. On the whole her frame of mind showed a marked divergence from the purring complacency of Attab, who was again curled up in his corner of the divan with a great peace radiating from every curve of his body.

But then he had killed his sparrow.

THE ACHIEVEMENT OF

THE CAT

IN THE POLITICAL HISTORY of nations it is no uncommon experience to find states and peoples which but a short time since were in bitter conflict and animosity with each other settled down comfortably on terms of mutual goodwill, and even alliance. The natural history of the social developments of species affords a similar instance in the coming-together of two once warring elements, now represented by civilised man and the domestic cat.

The fiercely waged struggle which went on between humans and felines in those far-off days, when sabre-toothed tiger and cave lion contended with primeval man, has long ago been decided in favour of the most fitly equipped combatant – the thing with a thumb – and the descendants of the dispossessed family are relegated today, for the most part, to the wastelands of jungle and veld, where an existence of self-effacement is the only alternative to extermination. But the *felis catus*, or whatever species was the ancestor of the modern domestic cat (a vexed question at present), by a master stroke of adaptation avoided the ruin of its race, and 'captured' a place in the very keystone of the conqueror's organisation. For not as a bond-servant or dependent has this proudest of mammals entered the human fraternity; not as a slave like the beasts of burden, or a humble camp-follower like the dog. The cat is domestic only as far as suits its own ends; it will not be kennelled or harnessed, nor suffer any dictation as to its goings-out or comings-in. Long contact with the human race has developed in it the art of diplomacy, and no Roman cardinal of medieval days knew better how to ingratiate himself with his surroundings than a cat with a saucer of cream on its mental horizon. But the social smoothness, the purring innocence, the softness of the velvet paw may be laid aside at a moment's notice, and the sinuous feline may disappear in deliberate aloofness to a world of roofs and chimney stacks, where the human element is distanced and disregarded. Or the innate savage spirit that helped its survival in the bygone days of tooth and claw may be summoned forth from beneath the sleek exterior, and the torture instinct (common alone to human and feline) may find free play in the death throes of some luckless bird or rodent. It is, indeed, no small triumph to have combined

the untrammelled liberty of primeval sav-
agery with the luxury which only a highly
developed civilisation can command; to be
lapped in the soft stuffs that commerce has
gathered from the far ends of the world; to
bask in the warmth that labour and industry
have dragged from the bowels of the earth;
to banquet on the dainties that wealth has
bespoken for its table; and withal to be a
free son of nature, a mighty hunter, a spiller
of life-blood. This is the victory of the cat.
But besides the credit of success the cat has
other qualities which compel recognition.
The animal which the Egyptians wor-
shipped as divine, which the Romans vener-
ated as a symbol of liberty, which Europeans
in the ignorant Middle Ages anathematised
as an agent of demonology has displayed to
all ages two closely blended characteristics
– courage and self-respect. No matter how
unfavourable the circumstances, both qualities are always to the fore. Confront a child,

a puppy and a kitten with a sudden danger:
the child will turn instinctively for assistance,
the puppy will grovel in abject submission
to the impending visitation, the kitten will
brace its tiny body for a frantic resistance.
And disassociate the luxury-loving cat from
the atmosphere of social comfort in which
it usually contrives to move, and observe
it critically under the adverse conditions
of civilisation – that civilisation which can
impel a man to the degradation of cloth-
ing himself in tawdry ribald garments and
capering mountebank dances in the streets
for the earning of the few coins that keep
him on the respectable, or non-criminal, side
of society. The cat of the slums and alleys –
starved, outcast, harried – still keeps amid
the prowlings of its adversity the bold, free,
panther tread with which it paced of yore
the temple courts of Thebes, still displays
the self-reliant watchfulness which man has
never taught it to lay aside. And when its

shifts and clever managings have not sufficed to stave off inexorable fate, when its enemies have proved too strong or too many for its defensive powers, it dies, fighting to the last, quivering with the choking rage or mastered resistance, and voicing in its death-yell that agony of bitter remonstrance which human animals, too, have flung at the powers that may be; the last protest against a destiny that might have made them happy – and has not.

NOTE ON THE TEXT

'Tobermory' was first published in *The Chronicles of Clovis* in 1911; 'The Philanthropist and the Happy Cat' was first published in *Beasts and Super-Beasts* in 1914; 'The Achievement of the Cat' was first published in *The Square Egg* in 1924. The text in this edition is based on the first edition of each story. In some instances, spelling, punctuation and grammar have been silently corrected to make the text more appealing to the modern reader.

NOTES

17 *The Envy of Sisyphus*: In Greek mythology, Sisyphus was condemned to push a boulder up a hill for all eternity, down which it always rolled again.

20 *Exchange and Mart*: A reference to the weekly paper founded in 1868 which ran classified adverts.

24 *Henley*: A reference to the Henley Royal Regatta, an annual rowing event.

25 *Mélisande in the Wood*: A reference to the 1920 opera *Pelléas et Mélisande* by Claude Debussy (1862–1918).

26 *Badminton Library… Punch*: The *Badminton Library* was a series of books about sport, published 1885–1902. *Punch, or, The London Charivari*, was a weekly satirical magazine published 1841–1992.

34 *ABC shop*: The Aerated Bread Company is best remembered for the network of tea shops it ran.

45 *the temple courts of Thebes*: Thebes was an ancient Egyptian city, and was the capital city from *c.*1550 to *c.*1290 BC. The reference is made as the ancient Egyptians famously revered cats, thinking them magical and lucky.